The Dragons of Wayward Crescent

Chris d'Lacey

The Dragons of Wayward Crescent

GRUFFEN

Illustrated by Adam Stower

ORCHARD BOOKS

For Lucy H – *hrrr!*

ORCHARD BOOKS
338 Euston Road, London NW1 3BH
Orchard Books Australia
Level 17/207 Kent Street, Sydney, NSW 2000

First published in 2009 by Orchard Books

ISBN 978 1 40830 232 3 (HB)
ISBN 978 1 84616 609 9 (PB)

Text © Chris d'Lacey 2009
Illustrations © Adam Stower 2009
The rights of Chris d'Lacey to be identified as the author
and Adam Stower to be identified as the illustrator of this
work have been asserted by them in accordance with the
Copyright, Designs and Patents Act, 1988.

All rights reserved.

A CIP catalogue record for this book
is available from the British Library.
3 5 7 9 10 8 6 4
Printed in Great Britain
Orchard Books is a division of Hachette Children's Books,
an Hachette UK company.
www.hachette.co.uk

Chapter One

"Mu-um!"

For the third night running, Lucy Pennykettle's startled voice came echoing out of her bedroom. Along the landing, in her workplace known as the Dragons' Den, Elizabeth Pennykettle put down her

paintbrush, wiped her
hands on her artist's
smock, and went
to investigate.

"Lucy, whatever's the matter?"

Lucy lay quivering under her
duvet. She had it pulled up so
tight under her nose that only her
head, her fingers and two bunches
of straw-coloured hair could be
seen. "It's here," she gulped. Her
gaze slanted towards one corner of
the room.

"What is?" said her mum.

"The monster," said Lucy, in
a muffled voice.

Mrs Pennykettle gave a quiet
sigh and sat down on the edge of the
bed. She rested her hands in her

lap and looked thoughtfully at her daughter. Lucy was only nine years old. She was a bright and clever child with a strong imagination. She loved stories and was fond of making them up. She could make up a story out of anything, in fact: a missing glove, a pebble on the beach, or even a shadow creeping up the wall...

"Lucy, we talked about this," her mum said. She pointed to a chink in the billowing curtains. Just beyond the open window, the light from the street-lamp in Wayward Crescent was glowing brightly through the sycamore trees, throwing criss-crossing lines and patterns into the room.

Lucy shook her head. "It's not branches, Mum. The monster flies. It jumps about. It's fast. It turns. It flits!"

"Flits?" Mrs Pennykettle asked, thinking that was an interesting thing for a 'monster' to do. When she was a child, monsters (or shadows) usually plodded through her imagination.

Lucy pulled down the duvet and went on in a fluster. "Sometimes it's big and sometimes it's small, on the ceiling and round the wall!"

"Very poetic," said her mum.

"I mean it," said Lucy, looking quite serious. "Close the window. Sew up the curtains. It might get in and steal me – or eat me!"

Mrs Pennykettle's gentle frown suggested she didn't think either of those things was terribly likely. She didn't think a monster was very likely, either. But it was unusual for Lucy to be quite so adamant. So, sweeping her red hair behind one ear, Elizabeth went to the window to check.

In the lamplight, the Crescent looked as beautiful as ever. Autumn was almost over and there was barely a leaf left hanging on the trees. A leaf was probably the culprit, she decided. One single piece of copper-coloured sycamore, fluttering madly in the wind, desperate to complete its seasonal cycle and fall into the road along with the others. She suggested this to Lucy, who replied rather sparkily, "Mum, I'm not scared of leaves!"

"Come and look," said her mum, not about to give up on her theory yet.

Nervously, Lucy came to stand by her side, just in time to see a large old leaf go dancing on the wind past the globe of the lamp.

"Now, quickly, turn and look at the wall," said her mum.

And sure enough, when they looked, there between the wardrobe and Lucy's mirror was a large, creepy, fast-moving shadow. *It could be a monster – if you were nine*, thought Mrs Pennykettle.

Lucy huffed and let her shoulders droop. She squeezed her pillow (which she'd brought out of bed just in case she needed any serious protection) and said, "But, Mum, I thought it had wings."

"Well, if it did," said her mum, guiding her back to bed, "it was probably an angel, come to watch over you."

And that was that. Lucy climbed back in, her mum kissed her goodnight and went back to the Den, and the house settled down into silence once more...for all of thirty seconds.

Then there came a yell so loud that Mrs Pennykettle squeezed on her clay too hard and gave the dragon she was making a silly squashed snout. She hurried back to find Lucy hidden under the duvet.

"What happened?" she asked, glancing at the wall. There was nothing to be seen.

But Lucy insisted the monster had returned. "I saw it, behind the curtains!" she shouted. "It had a tiny head and ears – and teeth!"

Mrs Pennykettle plonked her hands on her hips. "Right, there's only one way to deal with this," she said. "Grab your hot-water bottle. Tonight, you'll sleep in my room – and tomorrow..." She paused and played with her hair a moment. "Tomorrow, I'll make you a dragon."

The duvet rustled. Lucy's head popped out. "A special dragon?" she asked rather hopefully.

Her mother raised an eyebrow, which always meant 'yes'. "A very special dragon. A guard dragon," she said.

Chapter Two

Elizabeth Pennykettle had been making dragons from around about the time that Lucy had been born. She made other things, too – pots and mugs and decorative plates – but dragons were what she loved and dragons were what she was best known for.

Every dragon that came out of Liz's 'den' was moulded from a soft grey clay which had been dug from a quarry in the west of England, though its precise location was always kept a secret. A dragon could be found in every single room of the Pennykettles' house. They sat on windowsills, mantelpieces, tables and shelves. There was even one on the fridge in the kitchen and another – you would have to say 'fragrant' dragon – on the cistern of the toilet in the bathroom upstairs. Visitors to 42 Wayward Crescent could not help but touch and admire them.

They would pick them up and coo at them and sometimes offer to buy them. Often they'd remark how lifelike they looked. This always made Liz and Lucy smile, because they knew something their visitors didn't – but we'll come to that in a moment.

Everybody knows, or thinks they know, what a dragon looks like. In most people's minds they are scaly and fierce, with saliva dripping from their terrifying jaws. They have fearsome claws, sharp enough to tear through leather or wood. Their teeth are enormous and they breathe out fire. They are deadly and dangerous. People are usually quite frightened of them.

But the dragons of Wayward Crescent were nothing like the fearsome, scaly monsters that people usually imagine. Liz's dragons were friendly. Not cute, but charming. The kind of creatures you would want to take home to look after and keep especially dear to your heart. They all looked similar, but none were quite the same. Tiled green scales, spiky wings and oval-shaped eyes were their most common characteristics. Big flat feet and a curving tail were also popular, so that they could stand on a solid surface and look their maker – or their owner – in the eye. They occupied every shelf in the Dragons' Den, though most of them didn't stay there long. This was because every Tuesday, Thursday and Saturday afternoon, Liz would take some into Scrubbley, her local town, and sell them on a market stall. But occasionally – and it has to be said that this was quite rare – Liz made what she called a 'special' dragon. These were never sold. These were very different. These were...well, we'll come to that in a moment, too.

Special dragons looked the same as all the others. Indeed, anyone admiring the dragon with big ears which sat on top of the fridge in the kitchen would not have known it was a listening dragon, capable of picking up all sorts of noises, including human voices. Anyone passing the frowning dragon with a duster in its paws at the top of the stairs would never have guessed it was a snuffler dragon, which did a bit of cleaning when no one was looking. And the two impressive dragons that sat on Liz's workbench in the Dragons' Den, Gawain and Guinevere, had a very special role to play. But that we have to keep a secret for now. It's the subject of another story.

But how did it happen? How did Mrs Pennykettle make her dragons special or not? Well, there are as many mysteries surrounding Liz and Lucy as there are secrets about Liz's strange clay figures, but this is the time to reveal one of them.

Liz had a snowball in the fridge. That's right, a snowball. She had kept it since she was a little girl and it had magical properties – it could bring a dragon to life!

On the day she made her guard dragon for Lucy, Mrs Pennykettle did as she always did. She placed a generous wodge of clay on the turntable on her bench, smoothed it down with a small amount of water, then closed her eyes and let her hands glide around it. Like Lucy, she had a strong imagination. But it was something far more magical,

far more dreamlike, which guided her skilful thumbs and fingers to make the shape of her special dragons. Having said that, this particular dragon did come out quite ordinary looking. It was a 'he'.

A youthful, handsome 'he', with the usual spiky wings and big flat feet. But, and this was quite a big 'but', when Elizabeth opened her eyes to admire him there was something else there along with her dragon.

"What's that?" whispered Lucy, looking over her mum's shoulder. She pointed at something under his feet. It was common for Liz's special dragons to have some kind of object in their paws, but even Lucy had never seen one sitting on something before.

Liz leaned back and tapped her fingertips together. "It looks like a book," she said.

"A book?" snorted Lucy. She'd been expecting her guard dragon to have boxing gloves or a stick or at the very least scary teeth. A book! How was that going to protect her against a monster?

"Go and fetch the snowball," her mum said anyway.

Lucy scooted downstairs to the fridge. The snowball was in a plastic box in the bottom drawer of the freezer. Lucy's heart quickened as she picked it out. Neither she nor her mum truly understood the power of the ice inside this box. But what did that matter? It worked. It somehow put a spark of life into the clay. And today it would work again.

Lucy hurried upstairs and handed the box over. It was important that this part of the process be done quickly. For snowballs, even magical ones, can quickly melt in the warmth of the home (especially when the home is heated by dragons).

Liz prised off the lid. A wisp of icy vapour rose into the Den. In one or two places along the shelves, several dragons let out a *hrrr* of awe.

With the tip of her little finger, Liz broke off a tiny piece of ice and brought it into the open air. It glinted in the light of her anglepoise lamp. She handed the box back to Lucy, who immediately closed the lid. Lucy gulped and held her breath as her mum put the ice on the end of the dragon's snout. Within seconds the ice had melted and run inside his trumpet-shaped nostrils.

Mrs Pennykettle smiled and carefully twisted the turntable round, until the new dragon was facing the dragon called Guinevere. "Time to go," Liz said in a quiet voice, and guided Lucy towards the door.

From the doorway, Lucy took a quick glance back. Guinevere had opened her eyes. They were radiant and purple and shining with fire. Lucy clamped her hands to her breast and whispered, "Please make him the best guard dragon ever, Guinevere."

"Go," said Liz, softly but firmly.

And Lucy dared not argue. She blew the new dragon a heartfelt kiss and closed the door of the Dragons' Den.

Chapter Three

For the next two nights, Lucy slept in her mother's room. She was still too frightened to stay in hers and the new guard dragon needed to be kilned. Kilning was the process which made the clay firm and brought out the greeny-blue colour of the glaze. It took, on average, two or three days.

On the third morning, Lucy was settled at the kitchen table, colouring in pictures of woodland creatures, when the listening dragon twizzled its snout, looked down from the top of the fridge and went, *hrrr*.

Lucy sat up like a meerkat. She abandoned her pencils and went running down the hall. "Mum," she shouted. "He's done!"

Liz came out of the front room and together they hurried upstairs to the Den.

There, on the turntable, was a lovely young dragon, beautifully glazed. Guinevere's eyes were now closed again. She had gone back to her resting stance, with her paws pressed together as though in prayer. The new dragon's eyes were green and wide open, but as still and solid as the rest of his body.

Liz smiled and put her mouth up close to his ear. *Hrrr*, she went softly.

A puff of smoke came out of the dragon's nose. He shook his head, spluttered a smoke ring and blinked. When he opened his eyes again they were a brilliant shade of purple.

"Hello," Liz said in dragontongue – a forgotten language

that you and I would probably not understand, but any young dragon would.

"Gurrr," went the dragon.

"Is he growling?" asked Lucy.

"More like hiccoughs," said her mum. "He's just trying to find his spark."

"Gurrr-urr," went the dragon again. By now he had spotted the dragons on the shelves and his eyes had grown even wider still. He was either quite shocked or quite excited, but at that stage it was difficult to tell.

"What shall we call him?" Lucy whispered, anxiously biting her lip.

Liz tilted her head. "He's going to be a house dragon," she said.

"Neither yours nor mine. So we'll let him decide. We'll call him by the first word he speaks." She tickled the youngster under his chin. That seemed to do the trick. Half a second later, the dragon sneezed and made a sound that was like a cross between a grizzly bear growling and a dog huffing.

"Gurrr-uffen," he went.

"Gruffen." Lucy clapped her hands. "His name is Gruffen."

Liz smiled and ran her hand down the dragon's spine. "Hello, Gruffen. Welcome to the Dragons' Den."

Gruffen wrinkled his snout the way dragons often do. Above his eyes were two curved ridges, a little like eyebrows. Like eyebrows, they suddenly came together in a frown.

"He looks confused," said Lucy. "Say hello again."

Liz bent close to Gruffen's ear and said, "I'm Elizabeth, and this is Lucy."

Strictly speaking, it wasn't necessary for Liz to introduce them, for the new dragon had what is known as dragon 'auma'. In other words, he could share thoughts with the other clay dragons around him, all of whom knew Liz and Lucy, of course. But Liz did it because it seemed proper and courteous, and dragons, even very young ones, appreciate good manners.

Gruffen, however, still seemed puzzled. He flicked his tail and looked down at his feet. His ears pricked up when he saw his book.

"Ah," said Liz, "I think we're about to find out what that's for."

Gruffen stepped off the book and picked it up. It was an old-fashioned leather-bound book, in two bold shades of cream and brown. Etched in gold letters along the spine was its title, which Gruffen read aloud (in dragontongue).

"*Book of Dragon Procedures?*" Lucy translated. "Why does he need one of those?"

Liz hummed in thought. "Well, he is very young. He won't have had much…experience, I suppose.

Maybe it was asking a lot of the ice to send us a friendly guard dragon."

"Friendly?" sighed Lucy. "Mum, he's supposed to fight off monsters!"

They looked at Gruffen again. Still frowning, he turned his book over and blew dust off the

closed and ancient-looking leaves. When he opened it, Lucy was quick to see that it seemed to be some kind of dictionary, with sections marked out in alphabetical order. Gruffen flipped through the pages, A, B, C, until he stopped at D and the heading: 'Den, The Dragons'.

Lucy joined him and read the page out loud. "Dragons' Den: birthplace, sanctuary, home. To be guarded always, especially from persons not believing in dragons."

"Gosh, that's impressive," said Liz.

"Look up 'monsters'," said Lucy.

Hrrr? went Gruffen, who had no experience of monsters, of course.

"M," said Lucy impatiently. "Muh."

Gruffen turned to the section

marked by the letter M. There was nothing there yet.

Lucy threw up her hands. "How's he going to protect me if he doesn't know what to do?"

Hrrr? went Gruffen, obviously anxious that he'd failed before he'd even started. He flipped through his book to the letter G.

Surprisingly, there was an entry for himself. In dragontongue he muttered, "Gruffen: guard dragon. Tasks: to watch and learn and boldly protect."

"There you have it," said Liz. "That's the key. When you go to bed tonight, he'll be there to watch and learn. He needs to know what he's fighting before he can be a true guardian, doesn't he?"

"I suppose so," said Lucy, though she didn't seem convinced.

Gruffen hurred bravely and snapped his book shut. A pother of dust came out of the leaves, sending him into a sneezing fit.

Lucy rolled her eyes and walked away.

She could foresee another sleepless night ahead.

Chapter Four

For the remainder of that day, Gruffen followed Liz and Lucy around the house. There was much to see and learn. He particularly liked the kitchen with its view of the garden and he was fascinated by the spare room next to it, which was full of interesting bits of clutter. But on the whole there seemed to be nothing much to guard. The house was at peace, so were the dragons, and so for the most part were Liz and Lucy. At midday, there was one quick moment of excitement when some things called envelopes fell through a rectangular-shaped hole in the door. Gruffen immediately jumped on the envelopes and spiked the biggest with his tail to be sure it wouldn't cause any trouble.

Lucy, who was coming downstairs at the time, dryly announced, "Mum, Gruffen's killed a letter."

Liz forgave the young dragon, of course. She said the hole he'd made in the electricity bill was not important. He was just learning.

She said the same when the telephone rang and Gruffen pounced on the receiver and tried to fly away with it. (He ended up dropping it into a plant pot.)

Then at teatime there was a most dramatic incident when Liz spilt her cup of tea and scalded her fingers. Gruffen flew to the rescue. He roared at the tea and turned it into steam. The kitchen filled with brown-coloured mist and the smoke alarms went off.

"All part of his learning, I suppose," Lucy grumbled – once her ears had stopped ringing and she could see through the clouds.

For a while after that things were calm. But as the day wore on and it eventually became time for Lucy to go to bed, Gruffen began to tense his claws in readiness for his most important duty: protecting Lucy overnight.

Liz helped her into her pyjamas and told her a bedtime story. Gruffen enjoyed that. It was about a woman called Gwendolen who had lived among some creatures called polar bears. Surprisingly, Gruffen found an entry for them in his book. *Bears, polar. Large, furry and white. Guardians of the north. Friends of dragons. Wise to be polite to them at all times.* Gruffen decided he liked polar bears. Anything that did a bit of guarding was all right by him.

When the story came to an end, Liz brushed aside Lucy's fringe and said, "All right, time to sleep now. Gruffen will look after you."

Lucy looked doubtful. "Are you sure?"

"Oh, yes," said her mum. And with a brief hurr of dragontongue, she told Gruffen all about the 'monster' in the shadows.

Gruffen put on his fiercest frown and flew to the post at the end of Lucy's bed. Balancing carefully, he fixed his gaze on the corner of the room. Outside, the street lamp was already glowing. Liz said goodnight to them both and switched off the bedroom light. Immediately, a cluster of shadows touched the wall. Gruffen gave a start, then settled down into a crouch to watch them.

It was not a windy night, which was good in some ways, but not so good in others. Good because the shadows hardly moved at all, so Lucy wasn't frightened and fell asleep easily within ten minutes. But bad because Gruffen fell asleep as well. It was hopeless. The harder he stared at the motionless shadows, the drowsier he became. Before long, his eyelids had closed and his head had fallen forwards. Gentle hurring, snoring noises came tumbling out of his nose. His tail twitched gently as he dreamt of polar bears, and ice-white dragons, and—

"Arrgh!"

Lucy's squeal of terror woke him in an instant. He was so shocked, he toppled sideways off the bedpost. Two flaps of his quick wings righted him again. Outside, in the street, something was beeping. He had no idea what it was, but it was loud enough to wake a nine-year-old girl. It appeared to have woken the monster, too, for Lucy was shouting, "Gruffen, it's here! Do something!"

Gruffen snapped to attention. On the wall, one shadow was zigging and zagging at tremendous speed. Gruffen tried to follow it with his eyes, but there was no clear pattern to its flight and the sudden jerking movements made his neck scales rattle. He looked at Lucy. She was safe beneath her duvet. As far as Gruffen could tell, the shadow monster wasn't trying to attack her. It just seemed to be content to show off its flying skills. *Hrrr!* he went, challenging the thing to slow down and show itself. To his surprise (and slight worry), it did! Suddenly, the shadow grew large and wide and the monster spread a pair of spiky wings. It had a head that seemed too tiny for its body and ears that seemed too big for its head! Gruffen dived forward bravely, releasing a jet of fire from his throat. There was a crackling noise and a smell of burning! A long scorch mark appeared in Lucy's wallpaper.

But still the monster continued to dart.

Gruffen went after it. Although he was young and had much to learn, he had the auma of the other dragons to help him. Flying came naturally. Without thinking, he was able to alter his wing shape, twist his body, balance it with his tail and find speed in the muscles which flapped his wings. Soon he was flying as fast as the monster, copying its movements as though he were a mirror. Lucy said later that when she smelled the charred wallpaper, she had peeked out from under her duvet to watch. Gruffen was zipping about like a firework, she said – right up until the accident happened.

Oh yes, there was an accident, sadly.

Fast as he was, agile as he was, Gruffen was no match for solid objects. He was just about to roll

his body and release his second
jet of flame when he thudded
into the corner of Lucy's wardrobe.

Everything went black and he fell to the floor. The last thing he remembered before the dizziness overcame him was what he thought might be the smell of the monster. It turned out to be the smell of Lucy's socks.

He had landed inside her slipper.

Chapter Five

"No damage, only bruises," Gruffen heard Liz saying. He opened his eyes. The kitchen ceiling swam into view. It was daytime. He was lying on his back in Liz's hands. The last thing he remembered was chasing a monster. The monster! Where was it? With a shake of his head he jumped to his feet.

"Hey, hey, slow down," Liz said, catching him. She helped him up onto the kitchen table, where he tottered for a second and had to hold onto a banana in the fruit bowl for balance. He felt between his ears, where there seemed to be an extra bit of clay he didn't know about. It was shaped like an egg.

"You've had a bump," said Liz. "You've been asleep for quite a while."

Hrrr, went Gruffen, looking around. Lucy was sitting at the end of the table with her chin propped up in the cup of her hands. "Thanks to you, we'll have to redecorate," she said.

"Nonsense," said Liz. "It's only a small scorch mark. We can move the wardrobe in front of it."

Lucy flicked her gaze at Gruffen. The little dragon seemed slightly perplexed. "You burned my wallpaper," she told him.

"Not intentionally," said Liz. "He was doing what he thought was right." She tapped Gruffen on the shoulder. "Can you remember what you saw, Gruffen? Can you describe what this monster looked like?"

Gruffen sat on his haunches and blew a deep sigh. It was all coming back now. The zigging. The zagging. The sudden crash. Apart from that moment when he'd tried to fight it, the monster had had no shape at all.

He remembered the wings and the tiny head, though. Perhaps he could show Liz and Lucy that?

"It was like this," he hurred. Softening his scales, he stretched his wings until they resembled two flowing capes. Then he squeezed his head down into his shoulders and somehow produced two pointy ears as well.

Lucy gave a gasp. "Huh! He's turned into it!"

"So he has," said Liz, clapping his cleverness. "Now the mystery is solved. I know what it is. That's no monster. That's a—"

The doorbell rang before she could finish.

PENNYKETTLE

"A what?" demanded Lucy.

"In a moment. Let me answer the door," said her mum. "Now, Gruffen. You know what to do if visitors come into the house, don't you?"

To be on the safe side, Gruffen looked up 'Visitors' in his book of procedures. It said, *Visitors are welcome, but can become suspicious. Always be on guard. Act solid at all times or move quickly enough not to be seen by them.* He glanced at the listener on top of the fridge. It had already hardened its scales. Gruffen put his book away, flew onto a wall shelf and did the same.

"Good boy," said Liz and went to the door.

Moments later, a tall, elderly

gentleman came striding into the kitchen.

"This is Mr Bacon," Lucy said to Gruffen. "He lives next door." She had not forgotten the rules. She just liked to tease Mr Bacon now and then.

He twizzled his moustache and looked at her sourly. "Of course it's me. Who on earth were you talking to, child?"

"My guard dragon," said Lucy.

Her mother frowned darkly.

Mr Bacon cast a quick glance at Gruffen. On the whole, he didn't think much of the dragons or Lucy's love for them. "Strange girl," he muttered.

Lucy stuck out her tongue.

"Henry, why are you here?"
asked Liz, steering Mr Bacon round
to face her.

"Bats," he boomed. "In the attic,
Mrs P."

"Yes, I know," said Liz, in reply to his statement. "One's been flying around outside Lucy's bedroom window."

"Has there?" gasped Lucy. Her mouth fell open in astonishment.

On the shelf, Gruffen raised an eye ridge. He drummed his claws quietly against his book. Bat. Now he had a name for the monster. He needed to look that up. But how could he, with Mr Bacon standing right beside him?

"Need to speak to someone at the Council," said Henry. "Have them removed, before they breed."

"Breed?" asked Liz, glancing at Gruffen. The young dragon was hiding by an ornamental jug where he was quietly flicking through his book.

"Like rabbits," said Henry. "Hundreds in the rafters before you know it."

"Mum, they might bite me and suck my blood and turn me into a vampire!" cried Lucy, who knew a thing or two about someone called Count Dracula, who regularly turned into a giant bat.

"I don't think so," said Liz, wondering which was worse: Lucy's imagination or Henry Bacon's.

"Of course, we could just smoke them out," Henry said.

Which seemed to be a cue for Gruffen to snort a small puff of smoke into Henry's left ear.

He had just found an entry for 'Bats' in his book: *Small, harmless, nocturnal creatures. Many species are protected,* it said. Protected!

"What the…?" Henry wiggled a finger in his ear and turned round sharply to look at the dragon with the guilty expression and the open book. For a nanosecond of puzzled time he did ask himself if the model could have been a different shape the first time he'd seen it, but what was of far more importance was the strange sensation that the hairs in his ears had somehow been singed.

Liz moved quickly to right the situation. She picked up a tea cosy and dropped it over Gruffen and the jug.

Henry threw her a quizzical look.

"Too distracting while we're chatting," she said. She put her hand on Henry's shoulder and guided him down the hall. "Thank you for telling us about the bat, but I really don't think we need to do anything too drastic. As it happens, I know an expert in bat…technology. He'll sort it out in a jiffy, you'll see."

"Expert?" asked Henry, poking his ear again. *Why is there ash on my fingertip?* he wondered.

"Oh, he's the best there is," said Liz. And she pushed Henry out and came back into the kitchen.

Straightaway, Lucy echoed Mr Bacon's confusion. "Expert?" she said, with a twitch of her nose.

Liz lifted the cosy off Gruffen and the jug. The young dragon was blushing a deep shade of green. He blurted out what he'd found out about bats in his book.

"Exactly," said Liz. "It needs to be protected. And what better champion could it have than a guard dragon going by the name of Gruffen…?"

Chapter Six

That evening, Gruffen abandoned Lucy's bedpost and sat on her windowsill instead. By now, Lucy was not afraid. All afternoon she'd been poring over her wildlife books, reading up on anything she could about bats. She had discovered, for instance, that bats were mammals, just like people, and gorillas – and whales! They lived all over the world, she read, in caves and trees and even under bridges. There were mentions of barns and farm buildings too, but nothing about house roofs with loft insulation. For food, they caught insects: moths and the like. And – but this was something she knew now, anyway – they were fantastic at flying. Indeed, she stressed to Gruffen, bats were the only mammals that could fly.

At bedtime, she reminded Gruffen of these facts again. Being a patient, sensitive dragon he had found it interesting – the first time he'd heard it. By the tenth time he was beginning to wish that Liz would make a special lullaby dragon that could send Lucy off into a deep, deep sleep. But her mother soon did what mothers always do when children go to bed and stay awake too long: she came into the bedroom, took the book out of her daughter's hands, put it on the bedside table and said, "Head on the pillow now, please." Then she turned out the light. And that was that.

The moon rose over Wayward Crescent. From his windowside perch, Gruffen watched eagerly, missing not a rustle in the branches of the trees. Stars winked. Clouds and hours went drifting by. The night fell into silence, bar the distant hoot of an owl.

Then out of the black sky came a small shape. The bat! To Gruffen's delight, it darted twice around the globe of the street lamp then zipped back and forth in front of the window without ever once looking like it might crash into it. It was moving so swiftly that to anyone on the ground it must have looked just like a flying rubber ball. But Gruffen was able to quicken his vision and see that the bat had wonderful – if really quite delicate – wings. To you or I they would have looked like a kite stretched over thin wooden poles, but Gruffen could see that the bat had arms and fingers like a human. Like a mammal, in fact! When Lucy woke up, he would tell her that.

But for now, his mission was to find out more. He needed to know what the bat was doing here. He felt it was his duty, as a good guard dragon, to warn it not to stray too close to Henry Bacon's house. So he flew upwards to the open part of the window and launched himself into the night.

Almost immediately the bat came to join him. It whipped

around his head so many times that Gruffen felt quite dizzy at first. The bat was also trying to speak to him. It had a high-pitched squeaky voice, far above the husky tones of dragontongue. Every shrill little peep made Gruffen's ear scales sing. He tried to speak back, but the bat chittered in fear and flew further away, perhaps a little wary of the throaty growls. Gruffen adjusted his voice scales a little, until out of his mouth came a thin little *hrrr* that the bat did seem to understand.

"What are you?" it asked, flying closer again.

"A dragon," hurred Gruffen.

"A driggon?" said the bat, as it

went whizzing past. "I don't think I've met one of those before."

Gruffen cast his voice higher and repeated his words. It wasn't easy. The effort was making his tail point shake.

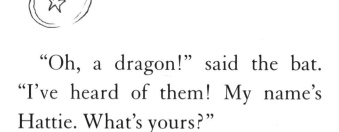

"Oh, a dragon!" said the bat. "I've heard of them! My name's Hattie. What's yours?"

Gruffen said his name and blew a smoke ring for her.

Hattie whizzed through it. "You can fly," she said, which seemed a bit obvious as Gruffen was as high as the gutters of the roofs. But he hurred and gyrated his wings a little, just to show that he wasn't held up by strings.

Hattie seemed pleased. "I like flying," she said. "Can you do this?" She dived towards a tree and performed a spectacular loop around a branch.

"I don't think so," Gruffen said warily, thinking back to his crash with the wardrobe. Trees, he was sure, would be equally as hard.

Hattie zoomed overhead and did an aeroplane dive. "I can teach you," she said, "if you know how to echo."

Hrrr? went Gruffen. He didn't understand.

"Echo," she said. "I go 'ping' at things and they ping back. I listen to the pings and they tell me where I should and shouldn't fly. Do you want to try it?"

Gruffen shook his head. In his opinion, pinging would be better suited to a listening dragon – of which he wasn't one. He flapped his wings and tilted back. "Why are you here? Are you lost?" he asked.

"No," said Hattie. "I'm just waiting to get in."

"In where?" asked Gruffen.

"To my roost," she said. "Do *you* have a roost?"

Gruffen thought about this. "I've got a window," he said. "I can get into that."

"Umm, that doesn't sound right," said Hattie. "Shall I show you my roost? It's just along here." And without another ping, she fluttered off up the Crescent, with Gruffen close behind.

Very soon, they came to a house with a framework of scaffolding poles outside. The top poles were reaching as high as the roof. It was on one of these that Hattie set down. Gruffen landed with an untidy wobble. The pole was slightly rusted, which made gripping its rounded surface easier. And this turned out to be very important, for

no sooner had Hattie put her feet on the pole than she fell back, hanging from it upside-down!

Gruffen gulped, held tight, and did the same. Surprisingly, it was quite a pleasant experience – once he'd got over the feeling that all his clay was rushing to his head.

"That's where I go in," said
Hattie. "Under there." She pointed
a wing at the eaves, the place where
the roof slates ended.

Gruffen looked across. He couldn't see an entrance, but Hattie was very small and could squeeze into most places easily, he thought. Which made him wonder why she was stuck outside at all. What was stopping her from going in? "How long do you have to wait?" he asked.

"I don't know," said Hattie. She pointed to a long white strip of plastic which ran all the way across the front of the house just behind the gutter. "I can't get in, because the people who mended the hole in the roof put that there. I've been waiting out here for days."

Gruffen raised an eye ridge, which made him sway gently.

(He tightened his grip and gave his wings a quick flap.) He looked closely at the plastic. It seemed quite fixed, which meant that Hattie might never get in. "Shall I try to burn a hole in it for you?" he asked.

Hattie squeaked gratefully, but seemed a bit concerned. "I don't think the people would like that," she said.

The wind blew, rocking Gruffen back and forth. He snorted a leaf off his nose and thought how Henry Bacon might react if he was the owner of this house and its plastic. Maybe Hattie was right. No burning. Not yet. "What happens if you don't go in?" he asked.

Hattie rustled her wings the way a person might shrug. There was sadness in her voice when she piped up next. "My batlets might die of cold," she said.

"Batlets?" said Gruffen.

"My babies," she replied. "They need to be born inside."

Gruffen frowned hard. This was worse than he'd thought. Bat babies? They would need serious guarding. "You could come and have your batlets in my roof," he suggested.

"Can I?" squeaked Hattie.

Gruffen blew a puff of smoke. Without looking at his book of procedures he couldn't be sure he was doing the right thing. It was that word, 'die', which convinced him that he was. But before he could say yes, Hattie was setting off.

"You live near the street lamp, don't you?" she peeped.

"Yes," said Gruffen, feeling giddy as he tried to fly upright again.

Hattie was by it in moments. "Is it this house?" she asked.

Gruffen blinked, dizzied by the glow of the lamp.

"This one's got a hole!" he heard Hattie say.

He looked up in time to see her fly under Henry Bacon's eaves.

"No!" he shouted and dashed in after her.

The streetlight faded and the blackness of Mr Bacon's attic consumed him. And then, *whumph!* He flew into something stringy, which caught in his wings and stopped them in an instant. Something wooden clattered down out of the rafters, narrowly missing his head. After that, the harder he flapped, the more trapped he became. Soon his feet and his tail became tangled up as well. He fired out a jet of flame, but it disappeared into the depths of the roof space, lighting it briefly, showing his predicament. He was caught.

Caught in a net inside Henry Bacon's roof.

Chapter Seven

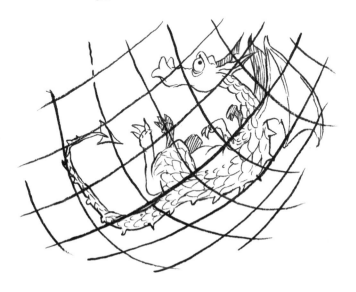

Almost immediately, Gruffen heard a shout from the room below the attic. He couldn't hear what words the voice was saying, but he could clearly understand the tone. It was Mr Bacon, sounding surprised. Any moment now, he would be coming up to see what was happening.

"Help!" Gruffen cried out to Hattie.

He heard her come swishing around his head. Amazingly, even in the dark of the roof, she could still fly brilliantly. "I think you need to practise your pinging," she said. She swooped over him and landed. He could hear her feet scratching on a nearby rafter. At least she was safe. But he wasn't. What would happen if Mr Bacon saw him in this net, even in his solid state? And Liz was going to be very angry. What could she say that would possibly explain the presence of one of her dragons here?

"You've got to get me out," he

panted to Hattie. "The man who lives here doesn't like dragons."

"Oh dear," said Hattie. "I'll try to bite through the net." There was a flutter and her feet touched down on his shoulders. Her body felt furry against his scales. "There's a lot of it," she said, tugging at the bits around Gruffen's ears. He heard it ripping and his nerves settled slightly, but not for long.

Suddenly, a door flapped back against the joists of the ceiling and a column of light appeared. Mr Bacon's head popped up through the hole. "Right, what's going on here?" He shone a torch around the roof. It flashed in Hattie's eyes and she gave her wings a flap.

"A-ha!" cried Mr Bacon. He was up his ladders like a March hare. "Bacon's bat catcher! Works a treat!" He fumbled his way across the ceiling, being careful to stand on the firm wooden joists and not the fragile plaster in between. His torch light wobbled around Gruffen's head. By now the young dragon had worked out a plan. Instead of flaming, if he spread his spark throughout his body scales and simply heated them up, perhaps he could melt the net? He felt sure it would work, but would he have time to do it before Mr Bacon reached this corner?

As it happened, he suddenly found plenty of time. Mr Bacon had stopped in the middle of the ceiling and was doing some kind of dance. This involved balancing on one foot and swinging his torch at an object flapping around his head. As the light sprayed about, Gruffen saw that the object was Hattie. She was dipping and swooping all around Mr Bacon, whose jigging was growing more demented by the moment.

"What the…? Get away! Be gone, you!" he was shouting.

And then his foot came down and
he went through the ceiling. Not all
the way through. Just one leg, all the
way up to his trouser pocket. He let
out a yelp that was rather like a
puppy dog having its first real sight
of a cat. The torch went out and
Gruffen broke free of the netting.

Hrrr! he roared to Hattie. And out they went, back the way they'd come.

This time, Gruffen flew straight home. He told Hattie to roost where she could that night, then he fluttered into Lucy's room.

She was sitting up in bed, shouting out for her mum.

Liz came in as Gruffen landed on the bedpost. "Gruffen, what on earth is going on?" she asked.

"I heard a crash!" reported Lucy. "From next door's roof!"

Liz stepped forward and took a piece of netting off Gruffen's tail. "Is this what I think it is?" she asked.

Gruffen nodded and told her all that had happened at Henry's.

"Right," she said, pushing back her sleeves (a sure sign of trouble). "I suppose we'd better go and help him, then."

"Help him?" said Lucy, looking put out. "He tried to catch Gruffen."

"Exactly," said Liz. "We have to help him understand that he doesn't mess about with my special dragons…"

Chapter Eight

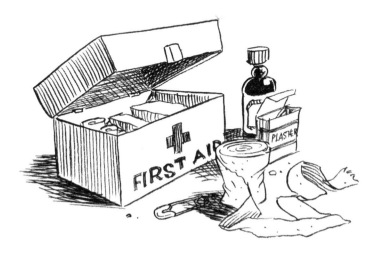

"But Mrs P," Henry bleated for the second time. "I wasn't trying to catch the bat. I was only trying to stop it from coming into the roof."

Elizabeth Pennykettle tightened her lips. "Henry, you know very well that Lucy and I don't approve of wildlife being harmed."

"But—?"

"I don't want to hear any bats – I mean, buts. Now, roll up your trouser leg and let me treat that gash."

"Mum, do I have to watch this?" Lucy said. She grimaced as Henry pulled up his trouser. There in the centre of his hairy shin was a large red cut, trickling blood – his reward for kicking a hole in his ceiling.

"No," Liz said. "You can bring me the bandage I've left in Henry's kitchen." She dipped a pad of lint into a bowl beside her and pressed it firmly against the wound.

"Ooh, ooh, ow!" went Henry,

shuffling his bottom against his seat as the antiseptic in the water got under his skin.

"Serves you right," said Liz. "What you did was dangerous, Henry. If that bat had been tangled up in the net it could have easily damaged a wing. You might have killed it."

"There was more than one of them," Henry grumbled, trying to establish a line of defence.

"No," said Lucy, "the other one was—"

"Thank you, I'll have that bandage now," said Liz, before Lucy could say a word about Gruffen.

Lucy's face reddened with indignation. "Well, you shouldn't

have caught him, anyway," she shouted, stamping her foot just so Henry got the message. "You're lucky that he didn't set fire to—"

"BANDAGE," said Liz, with a growl in her voice.

"Hmph!" went Lucy. She stomped into the kitchen.

"What is the child on about?" Henry said. "Bats are incapable of setting fire to anything."

"Good. That's just as well," said Liz.

"But something must be done all the same, Mrs P. What happened to your expert?"

"You nearly broke his tail!" said Lucy, coming back.

"I what?" spluttered Henry.

Liz pressed his wound again.

"Ow!" he yelped.

"Thank you. Now that I've got your attention," said Liz, "the expert will be visiting tomorrow."

"Will he?" said Lucy, looking rather puzzled.

"Yes," said Liz, wrapping a bandage round Henry's leg. "His name is Mr Greening and he knows about bats."

"Will he catch it?" asked Henry, twitching an eye.

"You'll catch it," said Liz, "if you touch that bat again. Ten, tomorrow morning. That's when he's coming. That's when our monster problem will be solved."

* * *

It was exactly ten o'clock when the doorbell rang at number 42. Lucy (holding Gruffen) answered the door. At first, neither of them could understand how the gentleman on the step could do very much to aid anyone, least of all a bat. He looked like an ancient garden gnome, thin and bearded with a multicoloured bobble hat on his head. There were cycle clips round both his ankles and a large blue rucksack on his back. Lucy thought at first he was a rambler who'd lost his way to Land's End, but when he cupped his hand above his grey, fizzy eyebrows she realised this could be him – the expert.

She and Gruffen exchanged
a wary look.

"Mr Greening?" said Lucy's mum,
coming down the hall.

"Mrs Pennykettle? Problem with
Chiroptera?" he said.

"No, a bat," said Lucy.

"I think that's what he means," said her mum. "Chiroptera is the Latin name for bats, is it not?"

"Indeed," said Mr Greening. "Fascinating creatures." He closed one eye and goggled at Gruffen. "Some people think they're related, you know."

"Bats and dragons?" gasped Lucy.

"Oh yes," said Mr Greening.

Lucy brought Gruffen up to her face. "Wow, you could have married Hattie!"

"Hattie?" Mr Greening looked a little puzzled.

Gruffen blushed, but of course the visitor didn't notice.

"Her name for our 'problem',"

Mrs Pennykettle said. "Ah, here's Henry, our next-door neighbour. He's been, erm, trying to solve the problem as well."

Henry limped up and shook hands with Mr Greening. "So, what's it to be? Butterfly net? Ultrasonic sound waves? Baited trap?"

"Henry!" Liz stamped her foot. "I'm sure Mr Greening's got a perfectly safe and acceptable solution, haven't you, Mr Greening?"

"Oh yes," he said. "Bat box. Up there, fixed to the sycamore."

"Box?" snorted Henry. "You're giving it a home?"

"Oh yes," said the visitor. He slipped off his rucksack and undid the flaps. Out of it he brought a pinewood box. It was the shape and size of a typical bird box, but had no hole, just an overhanging roof with a slit underneath, perfect for a bat to climb inside.

"Does anyone have a ladder?" Mr Greening asked.

Liz pushed Henry forward. "Mr Bacon has everything. Don't you, Henry?"

"I suppose so," he muttered, and went to get the pair hanging up in his garage.

Within ten minutes, Mr Greening had nailed the box to the tree. "Of course, there's no guarantee the bat will use it," he said.

"What?!" cried Henry.

"It takes time," said Mr Greening.

Liz ran a finger down Gruffen's back. "Oh, I think the bat will use it," she said. "Don't you agree, Lucy?"

* * *

That night, the moon was again full and round over the Crescent.

This time, it wasn't just Gruffen looking out for Hattie. Liz and Lucy were at the window, too.

Before long, they saw her flittering round the lamp. Away went Gruffen to speak with her. "I've found you a new place to roost," he said.

"Have you?" she said. "My batlets are ready."

"Over here," said Gruffen, landing on the box. It was shadowed by the trees, out of sight of prying eyes. Hattie landed beside him. She leaned over the edge of its roof to take a look.

"You'll never have to wait to go in," said Gruffen.

And sure enough, in she went.

"I like it!" Hattie said, with
an echoey peep. "Will you stay
with me?"

Gruffen looked across the street, to the amber lights of Number 42 Wayward Crescent. That was his home, his place to go in. His place to guard. His place to learn. "I can't," he said, "but I'll come and see you – and your batlets!"

"Thank you," twittered Hattie. "You're the best driggon I know."

"Dragon," Gruffen reminded her.

"Just teasing," she said.

Hrrr! went Gruffen, delighted that his mission had been a success. And off he flew into the night again…

Back home, to Lucy and the Dragons' Den.

Here's an extract from
the next story about

The Dragons of Wayward Crescent

GAUGE

Burning. Lucy Pennykettle could definitely smell burning. This was not unusual in her house at number 42 Wayward Crescent, Scrubbley. Lucy's mother, Liz, made clay dragons for a living, and as anybody knows, dragons breathe fire – well, some of Liz's special dragons did, anyway. The fires these dragons breathed were usually quite harmless. They took the form of smoke rings or breathy little hrrrs. But this form of burning, the one that was making Lucy's nostrils twitch, seemed to be coming directly from the kitchen. It smelled very much like toast to her.

"Mum!" she shouted and came charging down the stairs in her

pyjamas and hedgehog-shaped slippers.

Lucy's mum was on the phone in the front room of the house. She was chattering away "nineteen to the dozen" as people sometimes say and clearly hadn't heard Lucy or even smelt the burning. Still calling out to her, Lucy hurried on past and into the kitchen. Sure enough, there were two slices of bread toasting on a low light under the grill of the cooker. They were curling at the edges and turning black. Lucy balled her fists. Bravely, she ran to the cooker and turned off the gas. But as the jets of blue flame disappeared to nothing there was a gentle whumph and the toast itself set alight.

Lucy gasped and jumped back. "Mum!" she cried again. "There's a fire in the kitchen!" She glanced at the tall green dragon that always sat on top of the fridge. He was a listening dragon, with ears like rose petals. He put on a pair of small round spectacles and craned his neck towards the cooker.

"Do something!" said Lucy.

The listener sent out an urgent hrrr. Within seconds another dragon had zipped into the kitchen to land with a skid and a bump on the worktop. His name was Gruffen. He was a guard dragon.

Lucy sighed with relief. "Gruffen, put the fire out."

Gruffen studied the flames. The

scaly ridges above his eyes came together in a frown. Strange as it might seem, Gruffen had never actually seen a fire before. He was a young dragon, still learning how to puff smoke rings from the back of his throat. He could see there was a problem, but wasn't really sure what the solution might be. The toast made a cracking noise. A tongue of flame crept over the grill pan.

Lucy gave a little squeal. "Do something!" she repeated.

Gruffen leapt into action: he tapped his claws and consulted his book.

When Liz made one of her special dragons, it was not unusual for them to come with some kind of "magical" object. In Gruffen's case this was a book. A sort of manual of dragon procedures. A directory of things to do in awkward situations. He quickly looked up "fire". There were lots of interesting entries. Dragon's spark, said one, the spirit or life-force of the dragon, born from the eternal fire at the centre of the Earth. That made his eye ridges lift. Source of warming, said another. Used in cooking, said a third. And then there was a rather large entry in red: WARNING: fire can be dangerous to humans, but dragons may swallow it without fear (or hiccoughs). There was his answer. Gruffen slammed his book shut and flew to the grill...

More Orchard books you might enjoy

Billy Bonkers		
Giles Andreae & Nick Sharratt	978 1 84616 151 3	£4.99
Billy Bonkers 2:		
Giles Andreae & Nick Sharratt	978 1 40830 357 3	£5.99
Beast Quest: Ferno the Fire Dragon		
Adam Blade	978 1 84616 483 5	£4.99
Beast Quest: Sepron the Sea Serpent		
Adam Blade	978 1 84616 482 8	£4.99
Beast Quest: Arcta the Mountain Giant		
Adam Blade	978 1 84616 484 2	£4.99
Beast Quest: Tagus the Horse-Man		
Adam Blade	978 1 84616 486 6	£4.99
Beast Quest: Nanook the Snow Monster		
Adam Blade	978 1 84616485 9	£4.99
Beast Quest: Epos the Flame Bird		
Adam Blade	978 1 84616 487 3	£4.99
The Fire Within		
Chris d'Lacey	978 1 84121 533 4	£5.99
Icefire		
Chris d'Lacey	978 1 84362 134 8	£5.99
Fire Star		
Chris d'Lacey	978 1 84362 522 3	£5.99
The Fire Eternal		
Chris d'Lacey	978 1 84616 426 2	£5.99
Shakespeare Stories: Hamlet		
Andrew Matthews & Tony Ross	978 1 84121 340 8	£3.99
Shakespeare Stories: Macbeth		
Andrew Matthews & Tony Ross	978 1 84121 344 6	£3.99
Shakespeare Stories: Henry V		
Andrew Matthews & Tony Ross	978 1 84121 342 2	£3.99
Shakespeare Stories: A Midsummer Night's Dream		
Andrew Matthews & Tony Ross	978 1 84121 332 3	£3.99

Orchard books are available from all good bookshops, or can be ordered direct from the publisher:
Orchard Books, PO BOX 29, Douglas IM99 1BQ
Credit card orders please telephone 01624 836000 or fax 01624 837033
or visit our website: www.orchardbooks.co.uk or email: bookshop@enterprise.net for details.

To order please quote title, author and ISBN and your full name and address.
Cheques and postal orders should be made payable to 'Bookpost plc.'
Postage and packing is FREE within the UK (overseas customers should add £1.00 per book).

Prices and availability are subject to change.